WITHDRAWN

GOING APE

GOING APE
Jokes from the Jungle

BY LOUIS PHILLIPS
Illustrated by Bob Shein

VIKING KESTREL

For
Deborah
With admiration and affection.
Any person who has read as
many Phillips manuscripts as you have
deserves a badge of courage,
a medal of honor, a public thank-you.
L. P.

VIKING KESTREL
Published by the Penguin Group
Viking Penguin Inc., 40 West 23rd Street, New York, New York 10010, U.S.A.
Penguin Books Ltd, 27 Wrights Lane, London W8 5TZ, England
Penguin Books Australia Ltd, Ringwood, Victoria, Australia
Penguin Books Canada Ltd, 2801 John Street, Markham, Ontario, Canada L3R 1B4
Penguin Books (N.Z.) Ltd, 182–190 Wairau Road, Auckland 10, New Zealand

Penguin Books Ltd, Registered Offices: Harmondsworth, Middlesex, England

First published in 1988 by Viking Penguin Inc.
Published simultaneously in Canada
Text copyright © Louis Phillips, 1988
Illustrations copyright © Bob Shein, 1988
All rights reserved

Printed in the United States of America
by Haddon Craftsmen, Bloomsburg, Pennsylvania
Set in Trump
1 2 3 4 5 92 91 90 89 88

Library of Congress Cataloging in Publication Data
Phillips, Louis.
Going ape : jokes from the jungle / by Louis Phillips : illustrated by Bob Shein.
p. cm.
Summary: A collection of riddles, jokes, and puns about all kinds
of animals from aardvarks to zebras.
ISBN 0-670-81520-9
1. Animals—Juvenile humor.   2. Riddles.   [1. Animals—Wit and humor.
2. Jokes.   3. Riddles.   4. Puns and punning.]   I. Shein, Bob, ill.
II. Title.   PN6231.A5P48 1988   818′.5402—dc19

CONTENTS

CHAPTER ONE

Just When You Thought It Was Safe to Go Back into Another Joke Book

Alligators, Crocodiles, Sharks, Snakes

What do you call a sick alligator?
    An ill-igator.

Knock, knock.
Who's there?
Althea.
Althea who?
    Althea later, Alligator.

TEACHER: Ira, could you please use the words *defeat,*
    defense, and *detail* in a single sentence?
IRA: Certainly. De*feat* of the crocodile went under de-
fense before de*tail.*

HUNTER: How did you come to fall into that river
    filled with crocodiles?
SAFARI TOURIST: I didn't come to the river to fall in.

Knock, knock.
Who's there?
Hiss.
Hiss who?
Gesundheit.

THE CROCODILE SANDWICH POEM

Bread
Crocodile
Bread

HUNTER: I'll show you a crocodile if you don't
mind waiting for a while.
TOURIST: How long?
HUNTER: About eleven feet.

CROCODILE #1: Hey, did you see me in the movies?
CROCODILE #2: No. Were you in the movies?
CROCODILE #1: Sure. I starred in *Black Beauty*.
CROCODILE #2: You starred in *Black Beauty*? Are you
crazy? *Black Beauty* is the story of a horse.
CROCODILE #1: Some acting job, huh?

DEBORAH: What is a shark's favorite kind of candy?
RACHEL: I don't know.
DEBORAH: Jaws-breakers.

Knock, knock.
Who's there?
Hiss.
Hiss who?
Make up your mind. Are you a snake or an
owl?

SAD TALE: The nearsighted snake fell in love with the
garden hose.

FAY: What do sharks call swimmers?
SAM: I give up. What do sharks call swimmers?
FAY: Dinner.

BOBBY: What is dark brown, sweet, and dangerous?
IAN: I give up.
BOBBY: Shark-infested chocolate pudding.

SNAKE: Mama, I'm so glad I'm not a bird.
MAMA SNAKE: Why, son?
SNAKE: Because I can't fly.

How do some snakes call each other on the telephone?
They call collect, poison to poison.

What did the octopus say to the shark?
    One of these days—pow, pow, pow, pow,
    pow, pow, pow, pow—right in the kisser!

CHAPTER TWO

Roaring with Laughter

Lions, Tigers, Leopards, Cheetahs

ALBERT: What do you get if you cross a lion with peanut butter, two slices of bread, and a werewolf?

PAUL: I give up.

ALBERT: You get a hairy peanut-butter sandwich that roars like crazy when the moon is full.

ZOOKEEPER: Lady, run for your life. The lion has escaped from the zoo.

LADY: Well, I have nothing to worry about.

ZOOKEEPER: Why not?

LADY: It's a man-eating lion, isn't it?

SHORT-SHORT STORY:

    One lion, two hunters.
    One lion, one hunter.
    One lion.

What is white on the outside, yellow on the inside, and roars?
   A lion sandwich.

A man entered a clothing store and he saw a lion standing behind the counter.

The lion turned to the man and said, "I bet you're surprised to see a lion selling clothes."

"You bet I am," said the customer. "I didn't think the giraffe would ever sell this store."

IAN: Guess what. My father crossed a lion with a
         parrot.
MATTHEW: So what did he get?
IAN: I don't know, but when it talks, you listen.

SAM: Why are you wearing that green string around
         your finger?
FAY: To keep the lions away.
SAM: But there are no lions
         around here.
FAY: See how well it works?

NANCY: Do you know the difference
         between a dozen lions and a dozen eggs?
LAUREN: No, I don't.
NANCY: Then I'm not sending you to the store for a
         dozen eggs.

If a lion escaped from the zoo and came charging right at you, what steps would you take to escape?
   Long ones.

LION #1: Who is our most famous relative?
LION #2: It must be the Equator.
LION #1: How can it be the Equator?
LION #2: Well, everybody knows about the Equator.
LION #1: So?
LION #2: So. Isn't the Equator an imaginary *lion* that
      runs around the earth?

A lion was standing out in the middle of a field
going, "Baa, baa, baa."

The lion's mother approached. "What are you
doing, my son?" she asked. "Lions don't go 'Baa, baa,
baa.'"

"I know, Mother. I'm studying a second language."

What is orange, has stripes, and is red all over?
    A tiger with the measles.

MAMA LION TO HER SON CHASING A HUNTER: How many times, Junior, do I have to tell you not to play with your food?

BABY TIGER: Mama, was I born in Africa?
MOTHER TIGER: Of course not, dear. Tigers are from India.
BABY TIGER: Then I was born in India?
MOTHER TIGER: That's right, dear.
BABY TIGER: What part?
MOTHER TIGER: All of you, silly.

FEROCIOUS TIGER #1: Psst. I think I've found a way to escape from this cage and get away from this zoo. You want to escape with me?
FEROCIOUS TIGER #2: Are you kidding? I'm not going to go into the city's park at night. It's too dangerous.

JOHN: Did you know that there are no tigers in Africa?
ANN: No, I didn't.
JOHN: Well, it's true.
ANN: Then where are the Tigers?
JOHN: Well, today they're in Fenway Park playing the Red Sox.

DICK: What's the most unusual thing about African tigers?
EILEEN: There aren't any.

TIGER #1: Do you see that hunter over there?

TIGER #2: Yeah. What about him?

TIGER #1: He draws his pistol so fast that you never see the gun leave the holster.

TIGER #2: That's impressive. What's his name?

TIGER #1: No-Toes Brodie.

GREAT HUNTER #1: You see that tiger over there? I shot him with salt.

GREAT HUNTER #2: With salt? Why?

GREAT HUNTER #1: Because he was so far away when I fired my rifle that I had to do something to keep the meat from spoiling before I could reach it.

TIMOTHY: Mother, I just spotted a leopard.

MOTHER: Don't be silly, dear. Leopards are born spotted.

Once upon a time in India, there was a Raja who refused to kill the tigers that were destroying his village. Day after day, people were killed by man-eating tigers, but still the Raja refused to do anything. Finally, in desperation, the villagers rose up and overthrew the Raja and installed a new monarch on the throne.

It was the first time in history that a reign was called on account of game.

PETER: Which would you prefer—to have a leopard attack you, or a gorilla?

CONNIE: I would prefer to have the leopard attack the gorilla.

THE BEST WAY TO CATCH A LEOPARD

First, go to your local library and check out the most boring book that you know of. (Not *Going Ape*, we hope.) Next, get a fishing net, a telescope, and an empty peanut-butter jar.

Find yourself a shady and comfortable spot in the jungle and lie down to read your book. Obviously, since your book is so boring, you will soon fall asleep. When the leopard sees you sleeping, he or she will sneak up behind you and steal your book. Once the leopard starts reading the boring book, he or she will also fall asleep.

When you wake up, pick up your telescope and look at the leopard through the wrong end so that the leopard becomes very, very small. Toss your net over the leopard and then carefully deposit him or her into your peanut-butter jar.

And that's the best way to catch a leopard!

What do you have to know to teach a leopard to do tricks?
          You have to know more than the leopard.

DICK: Look at that beautiful stuffed leopard.
EILEEN: Where did you get it?
DICK: Oh, Seymour and I went to Africa for our
          vacation and we brought it back with us.
EILEEN: What's it stuffed with?
DICK: Seymour.

PAPA CHEETAH: Son, when I was your age I thought
          nothing of running 75 to 100 miles a day.
JUNIOR CHEETAH: I don't think much of it either.

What is orange, has spots, and comes in a red-and-white can?
          Campbell's cream of leopard soup.

JOHN: What weighs 2,000 pounds and flies?
AMY: I give up. What weighs 2,000 pounds and flies?
JOHN: Two 1,000-pound leopards.
AMY: But leopards don't fly.
JOHN: I know. I just put that in to make it hard.

DON: How do you make a slow cheetah fast?
COREY: Don't feed it.

JUNIOR LEOPARD: Mama! Mama!
MAMA LEOPARD: What's the matter, Junior?
JUNIOR LEOPARD: I'm seeing spots before my eyes.
MAMA LEOPARD: Silly! We're leopards. You're
          supposed to see spots in front of your eyes.

DOCTOR: Now just what seems to be the problem?
LEOPARD: When I look at my wife I see spots in front
          of my eyes.
DOCTOR: So? You're a leopard. You're supposed to see
          spots when you look at your wife.
LEOPARD: But I'm married to a zebra.

JOAN: Why do leopards hide behind trees?
RICKIE: To trip up ants?
JOAN: No. To keep the elephant company while the
          elephant trips the ants.

Which jungle animals are the least trustworthy?
          Cheetahs, of course.

Knock, knock.
Who's there?
Minerva.
Minerva who?
> Minervas wreck because that leopard keeps
> following me.

MOTHER CHEETAH: I just don't know what to do about
    Junior.
FATHER CHEETAH: Why? What's the problem?
MOTHER CHEETAH: He keeps chasing cars.
FATHER CHEETAH: So? A lot of animals chase cars.
MOTHER CHEETAH: Yes, but Junior catches them.

CHAPTER THREE

Monkeying Around

Apes, Baboons, Gorillas, Monkeys

BOB: What do you do if you're attacked by a killer ape?

ELYSA: I don't know. What do you do?

BOB: Use the buddy system.

ELYSA: The buddy system?

BOB: Certainly. When the ape attacks, throw him your buddy.

KAY: What do you call a small, kind, gentle, sympathetic killer ape?

JENNIFER: What?

KAY: A failure.

What is King Kong's favorite comic book character?
Little Orphan Banannie.

What is the best way to capture an ape?
Put on a yellow slicker and pretend you're a banana.

What did the banana do when it saw the ape approaching?
It split.

A famous movie ape invented a bell that rang every time a person scored a point in a game of table tennis. What was it called?
King Kong Ping Pong Ding Dong.

Why did the giant ape climb to the top of the Empire State Building?
Because it couldn't fit inside the elevator.

What is brown, hairy, weighs 2,000 pounds, and has a trunk?
A killer ape going on a vacation.

Not too long ago, a woman who was the head of her local library board decided to go to the movies. As she took her seat inside the darkened theater, she was quite amazed to see sitting in front of her a man with a baboon. The baboon was neatly dressed in a suit and he paid close attention to whatever was happening on the screen. The woman noticed that the baboon laughed at all the jokes, applauded the hero, and cried when the action turned sad.

At the end of the movie, the woman turned to the man who had brought the baboon with him. "Pardon me," the woman said, "but I couldn't help noticing the baboon. I can't get over how he seemed to enjoy the movie so much."

"I can't get over it either," the man said. "He didn't like the book at all."

Later that same afternoon, a man was walking down a street. He saw a baboon playing chess with a young boy.

The man stopped. He was amazed. "You know, I've never seen a baboon playing chess before. That must be a very intelligent baboon."

"Naah," the young boy replied. "He's not so smart. I've beat him two out of three so far."

SAM: Did you hear about the baby that drank gorilla milk for one week and gained seventeen pounds.

FAY: Wow! Seventeen pounds in one week? Whose baby was it?

SAM: The gorilla's.

Why did the giant gorilla climb to the top of the Empire State Building?
    To get its kite back.

    Two hunters were walking through the jungle when one of the hunters thought up a funny riddle. "Hey," he called out to his companion, "what's the difference between me and a gorilla?"
    "About forty yards! Run for your life!" his companion shouted back.

Where does a 2,000-pound gorilla sleep?
    Anywhere it wants to.

How do you get four gorillas inside a small car?
    Two in the front seat and two in the back
    seat.

What is the opposite of gorilla?
    *Stop*rilla.

*How many gorillas does it take to change a light
bulb?*
        Four. One to hold the light bulb and three to
        turn the ladder.

MONKEY #1: Where are you going with that suntan
        lotion?
MONKEY #2: I'm bringing it to a bunch of bananas.
MONKEY #1: Why?
MONKEY #2: Don't bananas peel in the sun?

How do you make a gorilla float?
Well, you take one gorilla, some soda water, and two scoops of vanilla ice cream, then put everything in a very large glass.

In what month of the year does a gorilla have the most fun?
Ape-ril.

JOAN: What time is it when a gorilla sits on your watch?
ALBERT: I give up. What time is it when a gorilla sits on your watch?
JOAN: Time to get a new watch.

What do gorillas eat for lunch?
Go-rilled cheese sandwiches, of course.

GORILLA #1: How do you get down from the Empire State Building?
GORILLA #2: You don't get down from the Empire State Building. You get down from a duck.

Why are gorillas large, brown, and hairy?
Because if they were small and white, they would be aspirins.

What is the name of the biggest ape in China?
Hong Kong.

MONKEY #1: You've got a banana in your ear.
MONKEY #2: What?
MONKEY #1: You've got a banana in your ear.
MONKEY #2: I'm sorry. I can't hear you. I've got a
       banana in my ear.

MONKEY #1: What happened to your friend the cow?
MONKEY #2: I don't speak to him anymore.
MONKEY #1: Why not?
MONKEY #2: Oh, he just talks *udder* nonsense all the
       time.

CHAPTER FOUR

Jumbo Jokes about
Large and Tall Animals

Elephants, Hippos, Rhinos, Giraffes

An elephant enters a doctor's office.

DOCTOR: What are you doing here?

ELEPHANT: I know that elephants are supposed to have good memories, but I have been suffering from amnesia.

DOCTOR: Hmmm. Tell me, how long have you had this problem?

ELEPHANT: What problem?

KATIE: What did the elephant say when it lost its trunk?

EVELYN: Tusk, tusk.

JOHN: Why don't they let elephants go to the beach?
EILEEN: Because they can't keep their trunks up.

ANNIE: What has four legs and flies?
MARYELLEN: Dumbo!

What weighs two tons and wears a glass slipper?
        Cinderelephant.

ELEPHANT BABY: Mama, what did Daddy say about
        elephants having good memories?
MAMA ELEPHANT: I forget, dear.

KIP: Why are elephants so wrinkled?
SID: Because they're too large to put on ironing
        boards.

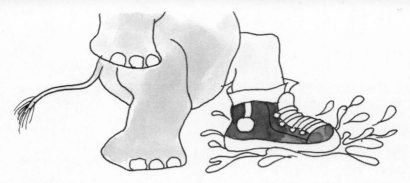

What goes thump, thump, thump, squish; thump, thump, thump, squish?
An elephant wearing a wet sneaker.

What's the difference between an elephant and the President of the United States?
About 3,000 pounds.

ARNIE: Why do elephants paint their toenails red?
NANCY: Why?
ARNIE: So they can hide in strawberry patches.
NANCY: I've never seen any elephants in strawberry patches.
ARNIE: That shows you how well it works.

WOMAN: This is my very first safari. How will I know if I trap a zebra?
SAFARI LEADER: It looks like a horse, is white, and has black stripes.
WOMAN: Suppose I see a tiger. How will I know?
SAFARI LEADER: It is dark yellow, almost orange, with dark stripes.
WOMAN: And suppose I come face-to-face with an elephant. How will I know?
SAFARI LEADER: By the smell of peanuts on its breath.

SAD STORY: The nearsighted elephant fell in love with
   a gas-station pump.

DEBORAH: What do you get when you cross an
   elephant with a fish?
RACHEL: Swimming trunks.

WENDY: What do you get when you cross an elephant
   with a skunk?
JOE: I don't know, but whatever you get, it won't have
   any trouble getting a seat on the bus.

ELEPHANT #1: I've decided to quit the circus.
ELEPHANT #2: Why?
ELEPHANT #1: I'm tired of working for peanuts.

Why do elephants have wrinkled knees?
   From playing marbles.

DOROTHY: What do you get when you cross an
   elephant with a parakeet?
LOUIS: What?
DOROTHY: The messiest bird cage in the world.

Hickory dickory dock,
The hippo ran up the clock.
The clock collapsed.

ELEPHANT: I don't care what they say about elephants,
        I'm beginning to suffer from severe lapses of
        memory. What should I do about it, Doc?
DOCTOR: Severe lapses of memory, you say?
ELEPHANT: Yes. I can't remember a thing from one day
        to the next. What do you think I should do?
DOCTOR: I think you should pay me in advance.

How do you make a hippopotamus stew?
        Keep it waiting for four or five hours.

DENTIST (TO THE ELEPHANT SITTING IN THE DENTIST'S
        CHAIR): Why are you crying? I haven't started
        to work on your tusks yet.
ELEPHANT: You're standing on my foot.

Knock, knock.
Who's there?
Noah.
Noah who?
        Noah any good hippopotamus jokes?

What always follows a hippopotamus?
        Its tail.

*What's the difference between a hippopotamus and a
piece of paper?*
        You can't make a spitball out of a
        hippopotamus.

What's gray, weighs more than 3,000 pounds, and comes in a bottle?
> Liquid Hippo.

IAN: What's the difference between a hippo?
MATTHEW: Between a hippo and what?
IAN: I'm not giving any hints.

What do hippos have that no other animals have?
> Baby hippos.

HIPPO #1: Did you take a bath today?
HIPPO #2: Gosh no. Is there one missing?

ELIZABETH: Why did the hippo cross the road?
SPENCER: It was the chicken's day off.

Why do hippos sit on marshmallows?
 To keep from falling into the hot chocolate.

What do you get when you cross a penguin with a hippopotamus?
 An animal in a very tight-fitting tuxedo.

CUSTOMER IN A RESTAURANT: Waiter, there seems to
 be a hippopotamus in my bowl of soup.
WAITER: Sorry, sir. I'm certain you were expecting a
 fly.

Why is the rhinoceros a humble animal?
 He doesn't blow his own horn.

TEACHER: Lauren, what's your favorite animal in the
    African jungle?
LAUREN: The hippopotamus.
TEACHER: OK. Please spell it.
LAUREN: I've changed my mind. My favorite wild
    animal is the lion.

LILLIAN: What is the plural of rhinoceros?
LOU: Why would anyone want more than one?

*How can you tell if there has been a rhinoceros in
your refrigerator?*
    Look for its footprints in the butter.

NANCY: Where do baby hippos come from?
LAUREN: They're delivered by very large storks.

CUSTOMER IN A RESTAURANT: Waiter, there seems to
    be a hippopotamus in my soup.
WAITER: Isn't it remarkable that I could even carry it
    to the table!

What is large, gray, and goes around in circles?
    A rhino caught in a revolving door.

TEACHER: How do you spell *rhinoceros*?
LESLIE: R-I-N-O-S-O-R-A-S.
TEACHER: I'm sorry, but that's not correct.
LESLIE: But you asked me how *I* spell it.

Why did the hippo sit down on a pumpkin?
    He wanted to play squash.

BABY HIPPO: Mama, how much is 5Q + 5Q?
MOTHER HIPPO: 10Q.
BABY HIPPO: You're welcome.

Why are giraffes such inexpensive animals to keep as pets?
    Because they make a little food go a long way.

ELIZA: What do you call the outside of a rhinoceros?
WILL: Hide.
ELIZA: Why should I hide?
WILL: Hide! Hide! The rhinoceros's outside.
ELIZA: So what do I care if the rhinoceros is outside?
    I'm not afraid of him.

FRED: How can you keep a rhinoceros from charging?
BENJAMIN: Take away its American Express card.

A giraffe walks into a clothing store to buy a necktie—
a long one. Unfortunately all the giraffe has on him is
a $100 bill. The clerk looks at the $100 bill, looks at
the giraffe, and thinks to himself, "Hmmm. Giraffes
don't know anything about money. I'll just give him a
dollar in change and he'll never know the difference."

The clerk rings up the sale and gives the giraffe a dollar
bill in change. "You know," he says, "we don't get many
giraffes in this store. In fact, as long as I've been working
here no giraffe has ever come in to buy a necktie."

"No wonder," the giraffe says. "At $99 a necktie I'm
not coming back either."

DEBORAH: What do you get when you cross a
         rhinoceros with a kangaroo?
IVY: I don't know, but whatever you get, when it hops,
     it leaves tremendous holes in your yard.

Why does a rhino wear blue sneakers?
    Because the red ones are at the cleaners.

*If a giraffe goes out into a rainstorm and it gets its
feet wet, will it get a sore throat?*
Yes, but not until a week later.

What is large, gray, has a horn, and hums?
An electric rhino.

LORNA: What's the easiest way to lift a rhinoceros?
TOM: Put an acorn under each foot and wait for them
to grow.

*What do you get if you cross a giraffe with a hedge-
hog?*
An eleven-foot toothbrush.

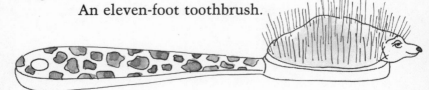

A mouse approached a giraffe. "What makes you so tall?" the mouse asked.

"The reason I am so tall," the giraffe answered, "is that I rub grease on the top of my head every day, and I rub grease up and down my neck."

The mouse looked puzzled. "I tried that," he said. "But look at me. It didn't work at all."

"What kind of grease did you use?" the giraffe asked.

"Crisco."

"Oh," replied the giraffe. "No wonder that didn't work. Crisco is shortening."

Where do giraffes rank on the evolutionary scale?
  Well, they are the highest form of life.

MAMA GIRAFFE: Eat your leaves, son. They put color in your cheeks.
GIRAFFE SON: Who wants green cheeks?

What's worse than a centipede with sore feet?
  A giraffe with a sore throat.

A lion and a giraffe enter a very elegant restaurant.
After the giraffe has studied the menu for a few
minutes, the waiter comes by to take their order.

WAITER: What will you have?

GIRAFFE: I think I will start with a bowl of tomato
        soup, and then I'll have your spinach omelet,
        some french fries, some corn, a glass of milk,
        and some vanilla ice cream for dessert.

WAITER: And your friend, Mr. Lion, what will he
        have?

GIRAFFE: Just bring him a glass of water.

WAITER: Are you sure he's not hungry?

GIRAFFE: Look, if the lion were hungry, do you think
        I'd be sitting at the same table with him?

CHAPTER FIVE

Winging It with Our Bird-Brained Friends

Parrots, Ostriches, Peacocks, Vultures

BABY OSTRICH: Mama, do ostriches really bury their heads in the sand when they're scared?

MAMA OSTRICH: Of course not, dear. That's just an old legend.

BABY OSTRICH: Then why do I have dirt in my ears?

Are you a parrot?

Are you a parrot?

Ah, come on.

Ah, come on.

Stop it!

Stop it!

I'm not talking to a stupid parrot anymore.

I'm not talking to a stupid parrot anymore.

What do you get when you cross a parrot with a centipede?

A walkie-talkie.

Two boys enter a pet store.

BOY #1: We would like to buy a parrot.

SALESPERSON: Certainly. Here's a nice one.

BOY #2: We'll take it.

SALESPERSON: Very good. Shall I send you the bill
            later?

BOY #1: Oh no. We're going to take the whole bird
        with us.

Two ostriches are standing around the ostrich farm
one day when a jet plane zooms overhead.

OSTRICH #1: Wow, did you see that? Whatever it is, it
            can fly without even flapping its wings.

OSTRICH #2: That's nice, but it shouldn't have to roar
            about it.

OSTRICH #1: What birds are present at every meal?

OSTRICH #2: Not ostriches, that's for sure . . . .Okay, I
            give up. What birds are present at every meal?

OSTRICH #1: Swallows, of course.

What do you get if you cross a parrot with a shark?
    A bird that talks your ear off.

Why do parrots always look so worried?
        You'd look worried, too, if you always had a
        big bill staring you in the face.

MARK: Did you hear the joke about the 50-year-old
          ostrich egg?
ANNIE: No, I didn't.
MARK: Oh well, it's a very old yolk.

A man goes into a restaurant. When he gets the
menu, he is surprised to see that there are two kinds
of soup on it.

    PARROT SOUP—50¢
    CHICKEN SOUP—$1.50

Since parrot soup is so much cheaper than chicken
soup, he tells the waiter he wants parrot soup. While
he is waiting for the soup to arrive, the customer feels
something pulling at his pants leg. He looks down and
there is a parrot. "Look," the parrot says, "order the
chicken soup and I'll pay you the $1.00 difference."

What do you get when you cross a parrot with a hyena?
      An animal that tells you what it's laughing at.

JOAN: Oh, come see the pretty green parrot.
KAREN: No thanks. I'll wait until it gets ripe.

What geometric figure should remind you of a lost parrot?
      Polygon.

KAREN: Did you hear the story about the peacock?
HANNAH: No.
KAREN: That's too bad. It's a beautiful tale (tail).

What's the difference between a vulture and a peanut-butter sandwich?
      A vulture doesn't stick to the roof of your mouth.

VULTURE #1: I know someplace where we can eat dirt cheap.
VULTURE #2: But I don't like the taste of dirt.

PEACOCK #1: Boy, oh boy, that wind last night—it blew down my tree and left only a few dead leaves in its place.
PEACOCK #2: Ah, a trade wind.

How many vultures does it take to change a light bulb?
            None. Vultures prefer to eat in the dark.

Two peacocks are sitting at a soda fountain when a giraffe enters, walks up the side of the wall, does a tap dance across the top of the ceiling, then waltzes out the back door.

PEACOCK #1: That was certainly strange.
PEACOCK #2: Naah. That giraffe never talks to anyone.

VULTURE #1: May I join you?
VULTURE #2: Why? Am I falling apart?

VULTURE #1: Let's go eat up the road.
VULTURE #2: No thanks. I don't like the taste of asphalt.

BABY VULTURE: Mama, should I take flying lessons?
MOTHER VULTURE: No. I don't want you taking crash courses.

FRED: What do you get if you cross a vulture with a kangaroo?
MARY: A bird that can put its dinner in its pocket.

CHAPTER SIX

From the Jungle to the Zoo

Animals of Different Stripes or No Stripes at All

What is black and white and green all over?
 A seasick zebra.

*What is black and white and green and black and
white?*
 Two zebras fighting over a pickle.

What is black and white and blue all over?
 A zebra lost at the North Pole.

KANGAROO #1: I don't feel well today.
KANGAROO #2: I feel kinda jumpy myself.

ZOOKEEPER: I can't stand the southwest corner of our
    zoo.
ZOOKEEPER'S WIFE: Why?
ZOOKEEPER: It's so noisy.
ZOOKEEPER'S WIFE: So noisy?
ZOOKEEPER: Sure. It's just yak, yak, yak all the time.

The cheerful old yak at the zoo
Could always find something to do.
When it bored him to go
To and fro, to and fro,
He reversed it and walked fro and to.

What is black and white and red all over?
    A zebra hiding in a bottle of ketchup.

ANTEATER #1: I hear there are a lot of ants in the
    watermelon patch.
ANTEATER #2: Watermelon patch? Is the watermelon
    leaking?

How do you pet a porcupine?
    Very, very carefully.

What is black and white and blue all over?
    A very sad zebra.

MATTHEW: Why did the zebra cross the road?
IAN: To prove that it wasn't chicken.

*What do you get when you cross a zebra with the
King of the Apes?*
        Tarzan stripes forever.

What is black and white and black and blue?
        A zebra that has fallen down a flight of stairs.

PAUL: What do you call a swami from Australia?
MINDY: I give up. What do you call a swami from
        Australia?
PAUL: A kan-guru.

NANCY: Why can't kangaroos wait for 1992?
LAUREN: Why?
NANCY: Because it's a leap year!

THE ANSWER IS: Out of bounds.
THE QUESTION IS: What do you call a very tired
        kangaroo?

JEAN: I just crossed a kangaroo with a racehorse.
PAUL: And what did you get?
JEAN: I don't know, but when it rains, the jockey can
        ride inside.

What did the grape say to the aardvark?
        Nothing. Grapes can't talk.

A SAD TALE: A nearsighted kangaroo fell in love with
a pogo stick.

SAFARI MEMBER #1: Are you planning on trying to
    ride that zebra?
SAFARI MEMBER #2: Yes, I am.
SAFARI MEMBER #1: Well, you're putting the saddle
    on backward.
SAFARI MEMBER #2: You don't know which way I'm
    going.

*What do you get when you cross an aardvark with a
tiger?*
    A very cross aardvark.

Knock, knock.
Who's there?
Aardvark.
Aardvark who?
    Aardvark won't hurt you, but all work and no
    play makes Jack a dull boy.

DEBORAH: What do you get when you cross a
     kangaroo with a sheep?
LOUIS: A wool sweater with large pockets.

FATHER KANGAROO: What's the matter? You seem
     nervous.
MOTHER KANGAROO: I'm not nervous. I just hate it
     when the children play inside.

TEACHER: Nancy, please spell *aardvark.*
NANCY: R-D-V-R-K.
TEACHER: What happened to the As?
NANCY: They moved to Kansas City from
     Philadelphia and finished second in the
     American League West.

Why are there no aardvarks in Hawaii?
>They couldn't afford the plane fare.

What is an aardvark?
>Aan aardvark is aan unusuaal aanimaal.

How is an aardvark like a brick?
>Neither one can play the trumpet.

Dear Professor Stevenson:

Could you please tell me if it is possible to tell the height of a building by using an aardvark?

A Serious Math Student

Dear Serious Math Student:

Of course it is possible to determine the height of a building by using an aardvark. Simply tie a string around the aardvark's tail, go to the top of the building, and gently lower the aardvark to the ground. Then measure the length of the string.

Professor Stevenson

WILL: An aardvark just crawled over my foot.
TONI: Which one?
WILL: How do I know? All aardvarks look alike to me.

BABY CAMEL: Mama, can I have a glass of water?
MAMA CAMEL: But why? Surely you can't be thirsty.
BABY CAMEL: Of course not. I just want to find out if
>my throat leaks.

BABY CAMEL: Mama, I have two belly buttons.
MAMA CAMEL: That's all right, dear. It's part of our
        country's Naval Reserve Program.

BABY CAMEL: Mama, which is smarter—a camel or a
        chicken?
MAMA CAMEL: We are, of course.
BABY CAMEL: How do you know?
MAMA CAMEL: Who ever heard of Kentucky Fried
        Camel?

BABY CAMEL: Mama, what walks over the water and
        under the water, and yet does not touch the
        water?
MAMA CAMEL: I give up, son. What walks over the
        water and under the water, and yet does not
        touch the water?
BABY CAMEL: A camel crossing a bridge and carrying a
        container of water on its back.

Knock, knock.
Who's there?
Anteater.
Anteater who?
        Anteater supper, but uncle won't eat a thing.

TEACHER: Nikki, could you please spell *anteater*?
NIKKI: Certainly. A-N-E-A-E-R.
TEACHER: What happened to the Ts?
NIKKI: I guess the golfer took them.

CAMEL #1: Where are you going?
CAMEL #2: It's so hot today that I thought I would go
       swimming.
CAMEL #1: Swimming? Are you out of your mind?
       The nearest ocean is about a thousand miles
       away.
CAMEL #2: Really?
CAMEL #1: Really.
CAMEL #2: This is the widest beach I've ever been on.

GARY: What has 4 eyes, 5 humps, 6 legs, 3 tails, 2
       bodies, and 3 ears?
JUDITH: I give up. What has 4 eyes, 5 humps, 6 legs, 3
       tails, 2 bodies, and 3 ears?
GARY: A camel with spare parts.

What should you do with a blue yak?
       Cheer it up.

A VERY SAD SHORT STORY: A nearsighted porcupine
fell in love with a pincushion.

LOUIS: What has 2 arms, 2 wings, 3 tails, 3 heads, 3 bodies, and 8 legs?
IVY: I give up.
LOUIS: A monkey holding a chicken while sitting on the back of a yak.

MARK: I can't find my yakcost.
ANNIE: What's a yakcost?
MARK: Oh, about $200 a pound.

What do you get when you cross a porcupine with a worm?
    Barbed wire.

What do you get when you cross a porcupine with an inner tube?

> A very flat tire.

There once was a hunter who was very fond of eating gnu meat for supper. He would eat gnu soup, gnu stew, gnu omelets, gnu hash. As long as it was gnu meat, the old hunter was happy. One night, however, there was no more gnu meat in the freezer, and so his wife had to serve him a pie filled with yak meat.

"Is this old?" the hunter asked his wife, as he took his first bites.

"Yes, but it's as good as gnu."

The zoo had two kinds of gnus: gnus that were fighting all the time, and gnus that were quiet and kind. "Obviously," the zookeeper sighed, "there's no gnus like good gnus."

BOB: What does a 700-pound ant say?
KAY: What?
BOB: Here, anteater. Come here, anteater.

What do you get when you cross a porcupine with a sheep?

> An animal that knits its own sweaters.